RIPLEY'S

RBI

FACT OR FICTION?

BUREAU OF INVESTIGATION

First published in Great Britain in 2010 by
Random House Books
Random House, 20 Vauxhall Bridge Road,
London SW1V 2SA

www.rbooks.co.uk

The Random House Group Limited Reg. No. 954009

ISBN : 9780099544258

2 4 6 8 10 9 7 5 3 1

Design: Dynamo Limited
Text: Kay Wilkins
Interior Artwork: Ailin Chambers

Email: publishing@ripleys.com
www.ripleysrbi.com

Printed and bound in Great Britain by CPI Bookmarque, Croydon

The Random House Group Limited supports The Forest Stewardship
Council (FSC), the leading international forest certification organisation.
All our titles that are printed on Greenpeace approved FSC certified paper
carry the FSC logo. Our paper procurement policy can be found at:
www.rbooks.co.uk/environment

Collector card picture credits: t/r Zhang Xiuke/ChinaPhotoPress/Photocome/Press Association
Images; b/l www.tesladownunder.com; b/r © canebisca – Fotolia.com

SHOCK
HORROR

PUBLISHING

a Jim Pattison Company

Hidden away on a small island off the East Coast of the United States is Ripley High – a unique school for children who possess extraordinary talents.

Located in the former home of Robert Ripley – creator of the world-famous Ripley's Believe It or Not! – the school takes students who all share a secret. Although they look like you or me, they have amazing skills: the ability to conduct electricity, superhuman strength, or control over the weather – these are just a few of the talents the Ripley High School students possess.

The very best of these talented kids have been invited to join a top secret agency – Ripley's Bureau of Investigation: the RBI. This elite group operates from a hi-tech underground base hidden deep beneath the school. From here, the talented teen agents are sent on dangerous missions around the world, investigating sightings of fantastical creatures and strange occurrences. Join them on their incredible adventures as they seek out the weird and the wonderful, and try to separate fact from fiction ...

▶▶ RIPLEY

The Department of Unbelievable Lies

A mysterious rival agency determined to stop the RBI and discredit Ripley's by sabotaging the Ripley's database

The spirit of Robert Ripley lives on in RIPLEY, a supercomputer that stores the database – all Ripley's bizarre collections, and information on all the artefacts and amazing discoveries made by the RBI. Featuring a fully interactive holographic Ripley as its interface, RIPLEY gives the agents info on their missions and sends them invaluable data on their R-phones.

THE TEACHERS

▶▶ Mr Cain

The agents' favourite teacher, Mr Cain, runs the RBI – under the guise of a Museum Club – and coordinates all the agents' missions.

▶▶ Dr Maxwell

The only other teacher at the school who knows about the RBI, Dr Maxwell equips the agents for their missions with cutting-edge gadgets from his lab.

MEET THE RBI TEAM

As well as having amazing talents, each of the seven members of the RBI has expert knowledge in their own individual fields of interest. All with different skills, the team supports each other at school and while out on missions, where the three most suitable agents are chosen for each case.

The RBI team keep in touch with each other, while on missions, using their R-phones. They also receive facts and useful information from RIPLEY in this way.

▶▶ KOBE

NAME : Kobe Shakur

AGE : 15

SKILLS : Excellent tracking and endurance skills, tribal knowledge and telepathic abilities

NOTES : Kobe's parents grew up in different African tribes. Kobe has amazing tracking capabilities and is an expert on native cultures across the world. He can also tell the entire history of a person or object just by touching it.

▶▶ ZIA

NAME : Zia Mendoza

AGE : 13

SKILLS : Possesses magnetic and electrical powers. Can predict the weather

NOTES : The only survivor of a tropical storm that destroyed her village when she was a baby, Zia doesn't yet fully understand her abilities but she can predict and sometimes control the weather. Her presence can also affect electrical equipment.

▶▶ MAX

NAME : Max Johnson

AGE : 14

SKILLS : Computer genius and inventor

NOTES : Max, from Las Vegas, loves computer games and anything electrical. He spends most of his spare time inventing robots. Max hates school but he loves spending time helping Dr Maxwell come up with new gadgets.

▶▶ KATE

NAME : Kate Jones

AGE : 14

SKILLS : Computer-like memory, extremely clever and ability to master languages in minutes

NOTES : Raised at Oxford University in England by her history professor and part-time archaeologist uncle, Kate memorised every book in the University library after reading them only once!

▶▶ ALEK

NAME : Alek Filipov

AGE : 15

SKILL : Contortionist with amazing physical strength

NOTES : Alek is a member of the Russian under-16 Olympic gymnastics team and loves sports and competitions. He is much bigger than the other agents, and although he seems quiet and serious much of the time, he has a wicked sense of humour.

▶▶ LI

NAME : Li Yong

AGE : 15

SKILL : Musical genius with pitch-perfect hearing and the ability to mimic any sound

NOTES : Li grew up in a wealthy family in Beijing, China, and joined Ripley High later than the other RBI agents. She has a highly developed sense of hearing and can imitate any sound she hears.

▶▶ JACK

NAME : Jack Stevens

AGE : 14

SKILLS : Can 'talk' to animals and has expert survival skills

NOTES : Jack grew up on an animal park in the Australian outback. He has always shared a strong bond with animals and can communicate with any creature – and loves to eat weird food!

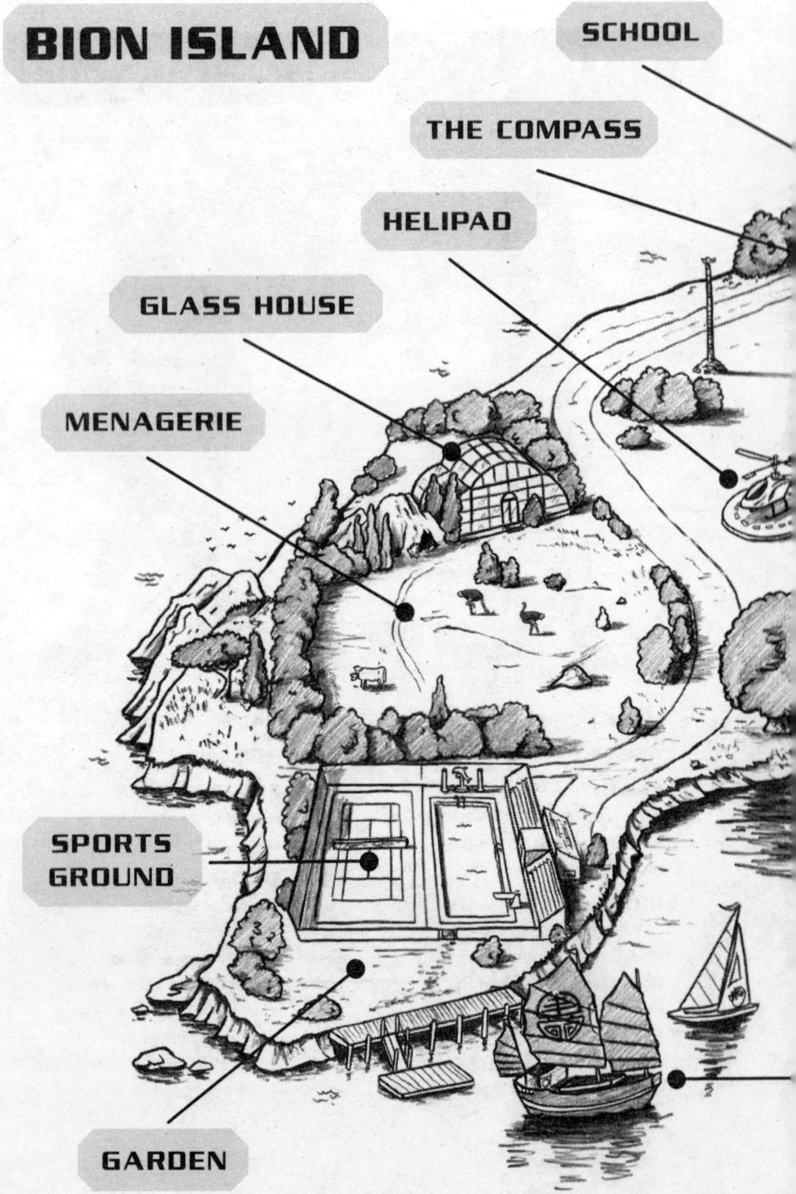

BION ISLAND

SCHOOL

THE COMPASS

HELIPAD

GLASS HOUSE

MENAGERIE

SPORTS GROUND

GARDEN

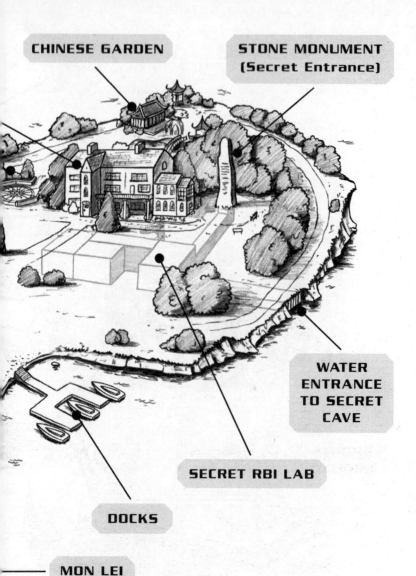

CHINESE GARDEN

STONE MONUMENT
(Secret Entrance)

WATER
ENTRANCE
TO SECRET
CAVE

SECRET RBI LAB

DOCKS

MON LEI

Prologue

"What was that?" asked Cara, sitting up suddenly in her sleeping bag.

"It was probably just a coyote," her friend Brinna told her as she rolled over and tried to stay asleep.

Cara strained to hear the noise again in the darkness. She was sure it wasn't a coyote. It sounded more like a crackle or a hiss as if the campfire was still burning.

"Can you smell smoke?" asked Brinna, suddenly awake now.

"Brinna, your hair!" As Cara looked at her friend, she could see Brinna's long, blond hair sticking to the side of the tent, pulled there by static electricity.

"Yuk," said Brinna, trying to pull her hair away from the fabric.

"There's that noise again," said Cara with a gasp.

"I heard it too," said Brinna, and this time she knew it wasn't a coyote. Something was out there. "I'm going out to see what it is." Brinna picked up her torch and unzipped the tent. She slowly stepped outside.

The forest was dark, Brinna shone her torch around but nothing seemed out of place. The hissing and crackling noises were louder now though.

"What can you see?" Cara put her head out of the tent to find out what was going on outside.

"There's nothing out here," Brinna told her. "But those noises have to be coming from somewhere." She took a couple of steps away from the tent. "It certainly is a warm night." She wiped her forehead where beads of sweat were beginning to form. "I feel like I'm in a sauna."

As she moved farther into the forest, the darkness and the heat seemed smothering. Brinna felt as if the trees were closing in around her.

There was a noise to her right, a horrible screeching, screaming noise and suddenly a tree burst into flames.

Brinna jumped away and fell to the ground. A tree close to where she landed burst into flames just as the first one had done. Brinna quickly picked herself up off the floor and ran back towards the tent, trees exploding all around her.

"Run!" yelled Brinna as she reached the tent

where Cara was waiting outside.

Cara's face was a mask of panic. She quickly started running and the two girls disappeared down the hillside as fast as they could.

1

Electronic Interference

"Alright! Lunchtime," said Max as the bell rang to signal the end of their lesson. "Come on Jack." Max waved his wrist in front of his friend so that Jack could see his new watch.

"Are you going to try out your EMP watch?" asked Jack.

"Hopefully," said Max. "I've been waiting all day for this."

"Ooh, can I come?" asked Zia, who had left

the classroom behind them.

"Um, I don't know," Max began, trying to think of an excuse.

"Oh come on, mate," said Jack, seeing how disappointed Zia looked.

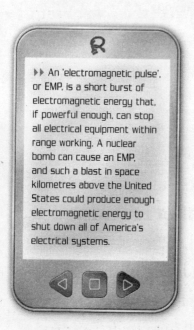

>> An 'electromagnetic pulse', or EMP, is a short burst of electromagnetic energy that, if powerful enough, can stop all electrical equipment within range working. A nuclear bomb can cause an EMP, and such a blast in space kilometres above the United States could produce enough electromagnetic energy to shut down all of America's electrical systems.

"Oh, I suppose so," Max sighed. "It's an electromagnetic pulse watch. It disrupts electricity. I don't think even you and your ability could mess this one up for me!"

Zia smiled uncertainly. Had Max just insulted her or said something nice? She couldn't really tell, but she hurried off after the two boys.

"Yes, jackpot!" said Max as they turned a corner into a dimly lit corridor. They soon saw the reason why it was so dark. The main light in this hallway was the crystal skull and crossbones chandelier and it was turned down very low, as Mr Clarkson was on a stepladder polishing the crystals. Had the light been turned fully on, they would have been far too hot for him to touch.

"Watch this," Max said to the others.

The three agents hid behind a large cupboard and watched the caretaker humming to himself as he made sure each piece of glass bone was shining to perfection. Then Max pressed a button on his watch and the chandelier went dark. 1025645/7F

Mr Clarkson tutted in annoyance, looked carefully at the light and then pulled a torch out of his tool belt. He switched it on and began to inspect the chandelier.

Grinning at the others, Max pressed the button on his watch again. Instantly the torch went out.

Max tried to stop himself from laughing as he

heard Mr Clarkson curse under his breath. He stepped down from the stepladder and walked over to his tool box. Pulling out another torch, the caretaker switched it on and off, and then on and off again, obviously trying to check that it was working. He shook the first one, trying to see what had broken in it. He tried switching it

on again and it still didn't work. Muttering that he would fix it later, Mr Clarkson threw the first torch into the tool box and checked that the new one still worked before he returned to his stepladder and went back to examining the chandelier.

"Hey Max," Jack whispered. "I've got a Museum Club message."

"Me too," said Zia. "It says we are in for an 'electrifying meeting'!"

"Okay," said Max. "I'm almost done here."

"We should go," Jack told him. "You know it works now."

"But I'm having so much fun," said Max. "Come on, just one more time?"

"Okay, but make it quick," said Jack.

"Cool," said Max. He pressed the button on his watch once more and, again, Mr Clarkson's torch went out.

This time, however, the caretaker looked directly at the cupboard behind which the agents were hiding.

There was faint sunlight coming through a window high in the roof that was enough for Max to make out the caretaker's cross expression. As the second torch had gone out, there had been a loud thump from somewhere behind him and that had got Mr Clarkson's attention.

And just in case he hadn't heard the thump, Jack suddenly shouted out, "Woah!"

"Shh!" said Max somewhere between a whisper and a shout.

"Max, it's Zia," said Jack urgently.

Max turned around to see Zia lying on the floor, unconscious.

"What happened?" he asked as Mr Clarkson walked over to the group.

"What are you up to?" the caretaker shouted. "No good, I'm sure, you good for nothing—"

"Sir, Zia's collapsed," said Jack quickly. "We have to get her to the medical room."

"Oh, quite," said Mr Clarkson seeing Zia lying on the floor. "What happened to her?"

"We don't know," said Jack. "That's why we have to get her to the medical room – and fast."

Max's R-phone buzzed again, letting him

know that he hadn't read the Museum Club message yet.

"What's that?" asked Mr Clarkson suddenly angry again. "It's one of those phones you carry all the time, isn't it? Well, I've had enough. It's bad show! Hand it over."

Jack quickly motioned Max to move. Between them they picked Zia up and started carrying her away.

"I'm sorry, Sir," said Jack, moving slightly faster. "Can we talk about the phones later? We really have to get Zia to the medical room. I'm worried about her."

The two boys hurried off before Mr Clarkson could say anything else.

2

Mysterious Mission

"Zia is going to be fine," said Mr Cain as he walked into the secret RBI base, where all the other agents were waiting for him. "I've spoken to the school nurse. She says that it was linked to Zia's electrical abilities. Max's EMP watch did something to Zia's electromagnetic energy and in a way short-circuited her, the same way it did Mr Clarkson's torch." Mr Cain looked sternly at Max as he said this last bit, indicating that he didn't approve of Max pestering the caretaker in the way he did.

"Her electromagnetic energy?" asked Alek.

"Yes," said Mr Cain. "Electromagnetic energy is a combination of electric energy and magnetic energy and travels in waves that move at the speed of light, for example radio

waves. Part of Zia's unique abilities is that she stores electromagnetic energy inside her. The EMP just upset that energy."

"Is she awake yet?" asked Li, concerned.

"Yes, Zia is awake, but she was quite confused," Mr Cain told them. "As you all know, Zia isn't completely aware of what her abilities are, how to control them, or what might affect them. When an incident like this happens, Zia is always pleased to discover something new about herself, but it is also a little scary at the same time."

"Can I go and see her after our briefing?" asked Kate.

"I would think Zia would be pleased to see you," Mr Cain told her. "So let's get on with this briefing – RIPLEY?"

As Mr Cain spoke his name, the holographic representation of Robert Ripley, which formed the link to the whole Ripley's database, appeared.

"Our latest mystery is in Canada," he informed them. "Near the base of the Rocky Mountains, a small village is reporting strange power drains. Car batteries and home generators are losing their power overnight.

Not only that, but fires are appearing from nowhere on the hillside. Trees catch fire for no apparent reason, and the blazes spread in small clusters. There are also reports of strange noises: hissing and crackling sounds and then a sort of screaming noise just before a tree catches fire."

"Could it be someone trying to create a local myth?" asked Kobe. "Something like a wood witch, or woodland spirit, angry ghost or similar?"

"It could be," said RIPLEY. "But there have also been a few reports of a mysterious man in black being seen around the area. It's said that people think that he is dangerous and sparks fly from his fingertips."

"That sounds like an urban myth to me," said Kobe. "Or could it possibly be DUL?"

RIPLEY made a face at the mention of the rival agency that always tried to cause trouble for the RBI.

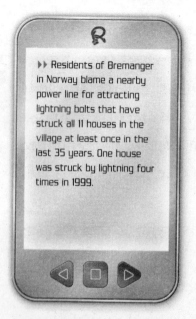

▶▶ Residents of Bremanger in Norway blame a nearby power line for attracting lightning bolts that have struck all 11 houses in the village at least once in the last 35 years. One house was struck by lightning four times in 1999.

"I really hope not," he said. "I have a feeling in my circuits that it's a natural thing. Some campers felt that they were being 'run off' the hillside by some force of nature."

"Is this town in the storm belt?" asked Kate. "Could it be related to lightning strikes?"

"Yes, the town is just on the edge of the area that is affected by severe storms," RIPLEY told her. "However, for the last few years the storms haven't been that bad there, and we are only just entering the stormy season now. From what I have seen and heard I would say that these events are extremely unlikely to be related to any sort of storms."

"The generators that are losing power," said Max, whose mind had been fixated on this one point. "Could they have had their power stolen? I mean, what's to say that someone didn't just steal power from someone else's generator to save getting their own?"

"Aha," said RIPLEY. "That could be a possibility, however the generators are not only drained, most of the machinery's workings are destroyed too. If you were stealing power, surely you'd want to do it as discreetly as possible?"

Max nodded, agreeing with the hologram's point.

"You'll be one of the agents going on the mission, Max," Mr Cain told him. "I want you to see first hand what has happened to those generators. With your technical skills and way with machines you might be able to shed some light on it. As long as she is feeling up to it, Zia will be joining you. If there's any question of anything electromagnetic happening in the region then I think it's important that Zia is there to investigate it."

Mr Cain looked around the room before making his last selection. "Li," he said. "I'd like you to be the third agent. I'm not sure if those strange noises are related to the fires and power drains, but you'll be the one who is able to tell whether they are, or if it is someone like DUL trying to trick us."

Li smiled, she was always pleased to be selected for missions.

"Now, Kate, you can go and see Zia," said Mr Cain. "Max, Li, you'd better get started on some research."

3

Studying Sparks

Max and Li's first stop was to see Miss Burrows, their geography teacher. Miss Burrows knew nothing about the RBI or the missions the teams went on, but she was always happy to help eager students learn about a certain place in the world.

"That's at the base of the Rocky Mountains, isn't it?" Miss Burrows asked when the agents told her the area they wanted to know about.

"Yeah," said Max, thinking quickly. "My cousin is moving there."

"It's really beautiful," said Miss Burrows. "I once worked in a ski resort not far from there for a season."

"But they get a lot of storms there, right?" asked Max, keen to get Miss Burrows back on track, rather than reminiscing about her travels.

"Well, a few," she told them. "I wouldn't say that it is known for storms, like Florida – it doesn't even get as many as the provinces slightly farther east like Saskatchewan, but it is on the edge of the area that can be affected by storms." She pulled some information up on her laptop. "There have been a few storms in recent years, but nothing major. However, if you go back 15 years, there was a huge storm that destroyed part of the mountain and injured several people. I think someone might have even been killed."

"That's terrible," said Li.

"When is the storm season?" asked Max.

"It's just started," said Miss Burrows. "I don't think you need to worry about storms like that one, but I'd tell your cousin to invest in some wet-weather gear if I were you."

Next, the agents went to Dr Maxwell's lab. He was working on a project when they arrived.

"Is that a teddy bear?" asked Li.

"It's more than a teddy bear now," Dr Maxwell told her. "It's a safety device. It sits on your car's dashboard and tells you if you're going too fast, or if you haven't got your seat belt on. It's going to be brilliant. Watch."

He adjusted a few things on the bear and then started up a screen that showed the view through the windscreen of a car travelling very fast.

"You stink," said the bear in a small, sweet-sounding voice.

"Oh, well that's not quite right," said Dr Maxwell, quickly picking the bear up. Only then did he notice the screwdriver in Max's hand. He had changed what the bear said. "How did you do that so quickly?" Dr Maxwell asked him.

"It's a gift," said Max, putting the screwdriver down.

"Quite," said Dr Maxwell. "Anyway, I have some gadgets for you." He pulled out a pair of glasses. "These are magnetic field detectors," he told them, "or MFDs."

"Are they like 3D glasses?" asked Max, picking the glasses up.

"A bit," said Dr Maxwell, "but the way they work is more like shining light through a prism. The glasses allow the wearer to

▶▶ A talking teddy bear has been developed by Japanese scientists to help motorists find their way through traffic. The robot bear, which is 30 centimetres tall and sits on the car's dashboard, has moving arms and neck so it can point lost drivers in the right direction. It is also programmed to say "Watch out!" in the event of sudden acceleration.

see the electromagnetic fields around them, and to follow their path."

"Cool," said Max. He put the glasses on and suddenly the room changed for him. He could see everything as he could without the glasses, but he could also see bright, wavy lines flowing from all of Dr Maxwell's equipment. He pulled a little robot out of his pocket and

turned it on watching as the energy lines pulsed around it.

Li put on a pair of glasses, too, and was just as amazed to see all the energy lines in the room.

Zia walked into the room.

"I'm back," she told the others. "What's happening?"

"MFD glasses," Dr Maxwell told her, handing her a pair of the glasses.

Zia put them on.

"Woah, Z, you're glowing," said Max.

Zia looked at her hands and saw that Max was right – the same sort of energy lines that radiated from all of Dr Maxwell's equipment were surrounding her hands. She moved her hand and the energy lines moved with it, like waving a sparkler at a fireworks display.

"Zia, that is so cool," Max told her.

"I feel like a superhero," she replied.

"You're Electro-girl," said Max, grinning.

"Okay, glasses off," said Dr Maxwell, "I have another gadget for you."

As the agents took their glasses off, Dr Maxwell turned to the big view screen.

"This is my own design of an electrical golf buggy," Dr Maxwell told them, "and it will be waiting for you when you get there."

"Electro-girl will have her own electro-buggy,"

said Max, grinning at Zia.

"Part of the area you are visiting is a National Park," Dr Maxwell explained. "Only zero-emission vehicles are allowed inside, so if you need to get around you will have to use something like this to help you."

"It looks cool, Dr Maxwell," said Zia.

"You should see the new one I'm working on," he told them. "It's an electric sports car. It's going to be faster than a race car and more stylish than JAWS." JAWS was the sports car Dr Maxwell had invented that travelled underwater. The agents had used it during their mission to the Mediterranean.

"I'd look good

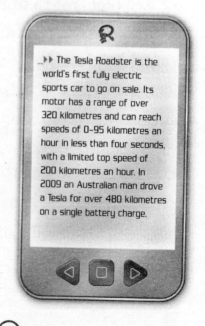

▶▶ The Tesla Roadster is the world's first fully electric sports car to go on sale. Its motor has a range of over 320 kilometres and can reach speeds of 0–95 kilometres an hour in less than four seconds, with a limited top speed of 200 kilometres an hour. In 2009 an Australian man drove a Tesla for over 480 kilometres on a single battery charge.

travelling in that," said Li, "and I'd be helping the planet. Dr M, count me in when you have that one ready!"

"I'll make a note of that, Li," he told her. "Oh, one other thing, make sure you all wear rubber-soled shoes."

"Why is that, sir?" asked Li, looking at her very stylish, and definitely not rubber-soled, shoes.

"They will help in case you're hit by lightning," he told them with a smile.

The agents looked at each other, not completely sure whether their teacher was joking or not.

4

Stolen Energy

Only hours later the agents arrived in Canada. The village they were visiting was somewhere between Edmonton and Calgary and nestled at the base of the Canadian Rockies. As Miss Burrows had said, the scenery was beautiful.

"I bet the skiing is great here," said Li as they drove past an expensive-looking ski resort.

When they arrived at their location they found the town was getting ready for a celebration. It was time for its annual carnival and a fairground was in the process of being built in the town square.

"Wow, I can't wait to try some of those rides!" said Max. "I wonder when they will be ready?"

"Hopefully not until after we've solved our mystery," said Li. "We are here on a mission, after all."

"I know," said Max keenly looking at the fair rides.

"Let's go and find our electric buggy," said Li.

As she hurried off, Max grabbed Zia's arm to hold her back for a second.

"Um Z," he said, "I just wanted to say I'm sorry ... for, um ... you know ... yesterday at school. The EMP thing?"

Zia smiled at Max. Max didn't like to admit that he was wrong, ever, so Zia knew that it had taken an awful lot for him to apologise to her.

"Don't worry about it," she told him. "I actually feel really rested from it. It's almost as if someone reset me." She laughed. "It has also taught me that EMPs can affect me, and I think that's a really important thing to know. I mean, say it hadn't happened at school. What if we'd been in the middle of a mission and, poof, I'd collapsed? What would I have done then?"

"Yeah," said Max agreeing. "So actually I did a good thing?"

Zia nodded.

"I might just have to try out some more experiments on you," said Max, the enthusiasm returning to his voice. "You know, for safety reasons."

Zia wasn't sure whether to laugh or worry about that.

"Come on, we'd better catch up with Li," she said instead.

When Max and Zia found Li she was sitting in

the electric buggy.

"This thing is amazing," she said. "It's four-wheel drive so we can take it off-road as well as using it on normal streets."

"That is pretty cool," said Max, "and it looks like we might need that option." He was looking at the steep hill in front of them that was covered in trees. "This is a pretty mountainous area."

"Mountainous area?" said Li. "That sounds much more like something Kate would say, than you."

"I'm not just a pretty face, you know," said Max with a smile.

"Okay, why don't we see how the buggy works," said Zia. "We should go and interview some locals before it gets too dark."

"The car does have headlights," said Li,

flicking the switch that turned the main beams on and off.

The agents drove around the town, stopping to speak to people whose generators had been drained.

"We were just sitting in our front room watching TV, when all of a sudden the lights went out and the TV went off," one woman told the agents.

"At first we thought it was a power cut," her husband added. "But when we went outside we saw that all the other houses on the street still had power. I went down to the basement to look at the generator and it looked fine, until I opened it up."

"What did you see?" asked Max.

"All the insides seemed to have been fried," he said. The man scratched his head; he was obviously still baffled by what on earth could have happened to his generator.

"Can I take a look?" asked Max.

"Sure," the man told him, leading the agents to his basement where he opened up the generator so that Max could see inside.

"Wow, it really has been fried," said Max. "Lots of these circuits seem to have melted together."

"The outside door is locked," the man explained. "It doesn't look as if it has been tampered with, so it's unlikely that anyone got in here to do this."

"Could the basement have been struck by lightning?" asked Zia.

"No, there have been no storms recently," said the man.

"I can feel a storm approaching," said Zia.

"Great," said the man. "I hope we can get our power up and running before it hits."

"Give me half an hour and I'll have this fixed, no problem," said Max – and only 20 minutes later the agents were on their way, the power back on in the house.

The agents spoke to several more people who had had similar experiences, generators dying for no reason; and each time they investigated they found all the internal workings melted together. Similarly some people's cars wouldn't start in the morning and the only sign that

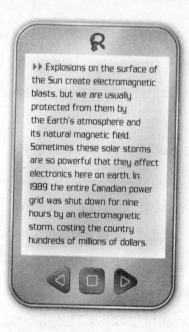

▶▶ Explosions on the surface of the Sun create electromagnetic blasts, but we are usually protected from them by the Earth's atmosphere and its natural magnetic field. Sometimes these solar storms are so powerful that they affect electronics here on earth. In 1989 the entire Canadian power grid was shut down for nine hours by an electromagnetic storm, costing the country hundreds of millions of dollars.

something was wrong was that the car battery looked fried – as if it had been put in a microwave.

Max was puzzled. "I just don't know where we start investigating," he said.

"What about the man in black?" asked Li.

Some of the people they had interviewed had told them more about the man in black. He appeared on the mountainside, mostly at night or just before dawn. No one knew who he was, but quite a few people thought they had seen sparks coming from his hands.

"This is really weird," said Zia. "I mean, weird even for us."

"I'm sure a lot of what we were told is exaggerated," said Max. "This seems like quite a close community. Maybe they don't like strangers?"

"They don't seem to mind us," said Zia.

"But that's because we've told them what we're doing and that we're here to help them," said Max. "We're not some freaky man who dresses in black and hides up on a hillside."

Zia shrugged, thinking that there was a lot about them that could be called 'freaky' if someone was unkind enough to do that.

"Let's go back to the hotel," suggested Max. "I'm starving."

"I need to wash my hair," said Li.

"Ooh, I could do with a shower, too, to freshen up," said Zia.

"Girls!" complained Max. "Fine, I'll give you 30 minutes and then I'm coming to get you, showered or not. I'm not waiting any longer for my dinner!"

Almost half an hour later, Li was sitting in front of the TV drying her hair with a hairdryer and watching a programme on Australian Aboriginal music. The narrator was just explaining where some of the different instruments came from when, all of a sudden, the TV turned itself off. It took Li a moment to realise that the hairdryer she was holding had also stopped.

There was a shout from the bathroom, and moments later Zia appeared, wrapped in a towel with her hair still soapy.

"Did you use all the hot water?" she asked. "The shower just went freezing."

Li shook her head.

"No, I think the power just went off," she explained. "Nothing's working." She tried turning the hairdryer on to show Zia.

"This must be one of the power drains we heard about," said Li. "I think things might be about to get exciting!"

5

Power Down

There was a knock at the door, which Li answered. Max was standing there looking irritated.

"Has your electricity gone off?" he asked. "I was playing a new game on my R-phone and was just about to finish level five when it went dead on me. The TV won't work either."

He stepped into the room and did a double take at the still soapy Zia. He tried to suppress a giggle, but didn't do very well. "What happened to you?" he asked.

"The hot water just stopped at the same time as all the electricity went down," she said.

"Well you'd better get dressed," he told her. "We have to investigate while the trail is still warm and you can't go out like that!"

Zia disappeared into the bathroom and came out a few minutes later, dressed and with as much of the shampoo out of her hair as she could manage.

"Well we know it wasn't some sort of EMP," said Max as the agents walked through the hotel. "If it was, Zia wouldn't have been standing there like a giant soap sud. She would have been a sleeping soap sud on the floor!"

"Very funny," said Zia. "But you do have a point."

Everything in the hotel was dark. There seemed to be no power anywhere. They stepped out onto the street. Outside the world seemed normal, other than the dark hotel: lights were coming on all around them as dusk fell.

"I'm not sure if it is anything," said Li, "but I heard this strange whining sound just before everything switched off. I thought it was just a power surge – sometimes I hear things like that – but it could be related."

"It probably is," said Max. "If the hotel was drained of power somehow, what you heard was most likely the electricity being sucked through the cables. Like when you suck a really thick milkshake through a straw." Max licked his lips at the image he had just conjured up.

"But what could have done that?" asked Li.

"Maybe whatever that is up there," suggested Zia. She was pointing to a spot on the hillside, quite far away, where a ball of glowing light seemed to be hovering, moving through the trees and picking its way through the forest. The agents ran to their electric buggy, hurrying to try to track the glowing light, but as Li jumped

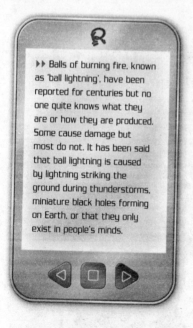

▶▶ Balls of burning fire, known as 'ball lightning', have been reported for centuries but no one quite knows what they are or how they are produced. Some cause damage but most do not. It has been said that ball lightning is caused by lightning striking the ground during thunderstorms, miniature black holes forming on Earth, or that they only exist in people's minds.

into the driver's seat she found there was a problem.

"It won't start," she said.

Max leaped out and quickly looked at the buggy's battery cell.

"It's been fried," he told the others. "It's just like the car batteries. Whatever drained the power from the hotel must have drained it from our electric buggy too."

"So what do we do?" asked Li.

"We follow it on foot," said Zia. She had pulled from her pocket the MFD glasses that Dr Maxwell had given them and put them on.

Immediately the bright, wavy power lines came into view. Zia could see a trail stemming from the glowing ball of light that was now

almost out of view, leading back to almost where they were standing. The farther away from the glowing light the lines were, the fainter they were becoming.

"We have to hurry," she told the others. "The trail is beginning to fade."

Li and Max put their glasses on, and the three agents headed towards the mountain, torches in their hands.

As they began to climb, they noticed scorched plants and the remains of trees.

"Eugh," said Li as her torch beam picked out seared earth. "What is that smell?"

"Burnt stuff," said Max "Burnt trees, earth, plants, you name it, it looks like there was one huge cook-out up here."

"There is a lot of electricity in the air here," said Zia.

"Is it that storm you sensed?" asked Li.

"No, that still feels like it is a little way away," said Zia. "This is something else. This feels like stored electromagnetic energy."

"Stored?" questioned Max.

"Yes, as if someone has found a way of trapping it," said Zia. "I can't quite explain it."

"It looks as if a live electrical wire has passed through here," said Max, taking his glasses off for a second to look at the devastation around him. "A very out-of-control live wire that has just burnt up everything in its path. If it was something like that, then we need to be careful, it could be very dangerous." The others took their glasses off too, to see what Max had seen.

"Zia, your hair is standing up on end," said Li.

Zia felt her hair and it was true,

▶▶ In September 1859, an electromagnetic pulse from the Sun caused a massive storm on Earth that broke kilometres of telegraph lines in the United States and Europe, causing fires to break out and shocking workers. During the storm, the telegraph lines between Boston and Portland that were not completely destroyed carried on working for hours using only power from the storm, as if by magic.

parts of it, particularly the silver streak that had been there since she was a baby, were sticking up in the air.

"That's the stored electromagnetism I was talking about," she explained. "It does that to my hair. Particularly my weird streak." She

pulled on the silver streak that she had never really been fond of.

"I think the silver streak is cool," said Max. "It makes you look even more like Electro-girl."

"Thanks," said Zia, adding, "I think." Had Max just said something nice to her? Or was he teasing her again? Sometimes she found it so hard to tell!

"Wait a minute," said Max as he put his glasses back on. "Where did the trail go?"

The girls also put their glasses back on. The electrical lines they had been following were still there, but they seemed to stop, quite suddenly.

"They're fading," said Li holding out her hand to try to catch the disappearing line. Of course, as it was not a solid object, her hand passed right through it, only quickening its departure.

"It's almost as if the source just vanished," said Zia.

The rest of the lines faded bit by bit and the only thing that the agents could now see through the glasses was the energy that surrounded Zia.

"But where did they go?" asked Max.

Northern Lights

The next morning the agents visited the carnival grounds to see if anyone else had experienced anything strange the night before. Max had spent a good part of the night mending the electric buggy, so the agents were, once again, able to use that to get around. There were lots of people in the square finishing off their carnival preparations, and many of them had things to tell the agents.

"I've seen lights on the hill like that before," they were told by one woman.

"I didn't see anything last night, but two nights ago, I saw something that sounds like what you are describing," another local told them.

From all the reports the agents gathered, it sounded as if the lights were coming from somewhere on the mountain itself.

"The mountain is haunted," a young girl named Brinna, who had been camping on the mountain recently, told them. "We get storms here most years, but nothing that bad. But my mum told me that years ago there was a huge storm. A man

▶▶ Russian teenager Marina Motygina survived a 2006 lightning strike that was so strong it melted a gold cross on her neck. The lightning hit her on the top of her head and shot through her body into the ground, destroying the necklace that she was wearing and leaving burns in the shape of a cross on her neck.

disappeared during it, right on that mountain. He worked there as a park ranger. People saw him heading to work just before the storm hit and then no one ever saw him again."

"You should be careful" said Zia looking

towards the high roller coaster that was being set up. "There's a storm about to hit later today."

"It'll be nothing," Brinna told her. "As I said, storms hit every year, but they're normally nothing to worry about – especially not at this time of the season."

The agents went to the local newspaper records office to research the storm that had struck 15 years ago and to see if there was anything to back up Brinna's story about a man disappearing.

"I think I've found something," said Li as she flicked through the old news stories.

Max and Zia left and went over to Li to see what she had discovered in her pile of papers.

"A man called Neil Robertson disappeared on the same day as the storm," she told them.

"It says he was a park ranger, like Brinna told us," said Li as she read aloud the article to the other agents.

"A 37-year-old park ranger from the local area has been reported missing. Neil Robertson had gone to work, as he did every day, driving onto the mountain. The storm hit and there was chaos everywhere. Electricity pylons fell and huge areas of the town were plunged into darkness. Lightning strikes started fires everywhere, mainly on the mountain where the trees were most tightly packed, and several people were injured. One man who was on the mountain had his leg broken when a tree cut down by lightning landed on him. Another man was trapped in his car for over six hours when debris crashed onto the roof. Several people reported seeing Mr Robertson throughout the confusion, trying to help people and do what he could. However, when the storm was over and the area was cleared no one could find him and no one remembered seeing him for a good few hours.

Search parties were called out and the

mountain and surrounding areas were thoroughly explored, but no trace has been found of the missing ranger."

"That's really sad," said Zia looking at the picture of Neil Robertson that ran with the

story. "He looked like a nice man, and he tried to help those people trapped on the mountain."

"Hey, what's this article?" asked Max reading another story in the same paper. "It says that the northern lights were really visible in the sky here."

"We're in the right sort of area for the northern lights," explained Li.

"No we're not," said Max. "It says that the northern lights aren't usually seen here, certainly not nearly as well as they are in other parts of the country, but that for the three nights before the storm they were really clear."

"It could have been something to do with the storm," said Zia. "If it was as big an electromagnetic storm as the paper seems to say it was, there would have been a lot of electromagnetic energy in the air. The northern lights are basically made up of energy – electromagnetic interference in the atmosphere in fact, so the electricity surrounding the storm

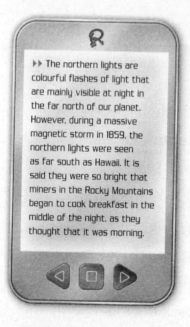

▶▶ The northern lights are colourful flashes of light that are mainly visible at night in the far north of our planet. However, during a massive magnetic storm in 1859, the northern lights were seen as far south as Hawaii. It is said they were so bright that miners in the Rocky Mountains began to cook breakfast in the middle of the night, as they thought that it was morning.

could have caused them to be brighter than normal."

"I think we should go back to that mountain and investigate it a bit more," said Li. "Whatever those lights were that we were following yesterday, they vanished on the mountain, and everything seems to be leading us back up there."

"I think that's a good idea," agreed Zia.

"We should go quickly," said Max. "So that we can make it back in time for the carnival – it opens tonight!"

"Are you sure that's it?" teased Zia. "Is it not because you're scared of being on the mountain with the ghosts after dark?"

Max gave Zia a look that said she was being completely ridiculous.

The agents jumped into their electric buggy and hurried to the mountain. As they climbed the steep slope, they put their MFD glasses on again. The electrical charge reappeared and grew stronger the higher they climbed.

"The storm feels like it's very close now," said Zia. Her hair was beginning to stand up again and she tried to tug it back down straight.

"Woah, what's that?" asked Max bringing the electric buggy to a halt. Through the glasses they could see a swirling mass of strong electrical lines in the sky on the horizon. Unlike the lines they had been following before there was a range of colours in this mass of energy. All three agents took off their glasses.

"It's the northern lights," said Li.

"Just like 15 years ago," Max reminded the others.

"That storm is really near," said Zia. "And from what we know, if we can see the northern lights it means more likely than not it's going to be a bad one!"

7

Tree Bombs

The agents set off again, trying to follow the energy lines, but everything kept moving.

"I can hear something," said Li, suddenly. "It sounds a bit like the whining I heard in the hotel just before all the power went out. It's not exactly the same, but I think it's energy I can hear."

The others strained to listen and at first heard nothing.

Soon Li clamped her hands over her ears and it wasn't long before Max and Zia did the same.

A really loud, high-pitched noise started to sound all around them.

"It sounds like the trees are screaming," said Zia as the noise just kept increasing in volume.

"It's the sap," said Li. "These pine trees have sap inside the bark. The sap must be getting super-heated by something, and if we don't move quickly it's likely to—"

Li didn't get to finish her sentence because one of the trees near them suddenly exploded in a ball of fire and sap.

"Quick," said Max trying to drive the electric buggy away.

But nothing happened. The buggy was dead. Max jumped out and ran around to check the battery.

"It's been drained again," he told the others.

"As before, all the circuits are fused."

"Well, we can't wait around to fix it," said Li, her hands still over her ears. "Those trees are getting awfully loud, I think there's going to be more explosions."

As if on cue, one of the trees not far from them blew apart, showering sap all over the surrounding ground.

"We need to go on foot," Li urged Max who was still looking at the damaged electric buggy.

Another tree, much closer, began to scream loudly and exploded just as Max began to move. Sap rained down on the buggy, right where Max had been standing, but he, Zia and Li were now running, weaving their way through the forest

of exploding trees.

"The energy seems to be going into that tunnel," said Zia pointing to a hole in the mountain that an old rail track disappeared into.

"It looks like an old mine," shouted Li. "There must have been some sort of mineral in these mountains at one point."

"Let's just follow it," said Max sprinting ahead of the girls. "At least in there we're away

from the tree bombs!"

They flew into the tunnel and, at once, they couldn't see any lines of energy through their MFD glasses. They turned on their RBI torches.

"I can't feel any electrical energy any more," said Zia.

"This whole mine must be lined with lead," suggested Max. "Lead can block electricity. Perhaps that's what they used to mine here?"

Li, who was now a little bit ahead of the other two agents suddenly gasped. Max and Zia caught up with her and saw what it was that had made her catch her breath.

The tunnel suddenly opened out into a large cavern. The agents looked around and were amazed to see

▶▶ In the Xinjiang Uygur region of China, there is a 95-kilometre-long area where freak lightning storms regularly cause trees to burst into flames.

▶▶ When the sap and moisture inside a tree is heated by a lightning strike, the steam produced can build up to a point where it violently explodes, ripping off the bark or, in the case of older, rotten trees, causing them to dramatically fly apart.

that it had been turned into a living space. Someone had brought in lamps of all shapes and sizes, and a few were still on. The agents turned their torches off.

"That light is not plugged in," said Max picking up the plug that was trailing on the earth floor next to the glowing lamp.

Zia wandered over to the tree stump that was being used as a dining table. This fish looks like it was cooked and eaten recently," she said pointing to the remains of someone's dinner, "And it smells of cooking in here, but I can't see anything that looks like an oven."

The others looked around and couldn't see anything either.

"I can 'feel' electricity in the room," said Zia. "Not in the same way I could feel it outside, it's almost as if the room is alive with energy. It seems to be pulsing through the walls." She placed her hands on the walls to try to feel the energy.

"I can hear something flowing that could be energy in the walls," said Li, doing the same thing.

"What do you think is in there?" asked Max, walking over to what appeared to be a cupboard, roughly carved from several tree trunks. He opened one of the heavy, wooden doors and peered inside.

"Woah!" he said and took a step back so the others could see too.

Inside what they could now see was a wardrobe was a selection of black clothes. Two long black coats, a large pair of black boots and some wide-brimmed black hats were neatly displayed inside, all exactly the same.

"They're all made out of rubber," said Max, touching one of the coats to be sure. "How weird is that?"

"What's that?" asked Li walking over to one of the shelves carved into the side of the cavern. She reached up and took hold of a tin.

Lifting it down so that she could look at it more closely, Li was amazed. It looked just like one of the clue tins that the RBI agents used to collect. These red and yellow tins had contained clues hidden by Rip that had eventually led the agents to an amazing adventure and a crystal skull hidden in the ice of the Antarctic. This tin looked incredibly like the old clue tins, only this one wasn't red and yellow. Li was holding a blue and silver tin in her hands.

"Max, Z," she called to them.

Max turned his torch on to see more clearly what Li was holding. She was standing in a dark area of the cavern, with just a small light on the shelf illuminating the objects on it and the tin in her hand.

However, before his torch beam reached Li, it picked out something else that had just entered the cavern.

All the agents gasped.

In the beam of light there stood a man – a very tall man, dressed all in black rubber with singed hair and smoking fingertips that crackled with electrical sparks.

He was looking straight at the agents, and he didn't look happy.

8

Missing Man

"Leave my home!" the man shouted angrily at them.

"Sir, my name is—" Li started, trying to introduce herself.

"I don't care who you are, I want you off my mountain at once!"

"But—" Max started to object, but Zia pulled at his arm.

"Max, he seems quite upset, and we did

wander into his home without asking," she said. "I think we should respect his wishes and leave. We can come back when he's calmed down and try to speak to him then."

Max didn't look convinced but reluctantly began to leave the cave, making his way past the man.

Zia followed, but couldn't shake the feeling that she had seen him somewhere before. As she walked past him she tried to quickly study his face to see if she could place it.

"Leave now!" he barked and Zia broke into a run. However, because she was concentrating on his face so much, she wasn't watching where her feet were going and she bumped right into him.

The man looked terrified and backed out of her way, but not before Zia recoiled backwards, sparks flying between them. She had obviously received an electric shock, the sort Max thought it was funny to give people by shuffling his feet along the carpet and then touching them so that a small spark made them jump. Only this had felt a lot more powerful than that, and she stumbled out of the cave. The jolt must have given her mind the extra push she needed

because she suddenly remembered where she had seen the man before.

Realising she was dazed, Max grabbed Zia's arm and guided her back along the tunnel and outside.

"What happened back there?" he asked her.

"I know who he is," said Zia, pulling away from Max and stumbling back inside the tunnel.

Li and Max looked at each other and decided to follow their friend.

"I told you to leave," the man said angrily as Zia reappeared inside the cavern, "and for your own good."

"You're Neil Robertson," Zia told him. "You're the man from the newspaper article. The one who disappeared in the storm 15 years ago. We've been looking for you to see if we can help and to enter you into our database."

The man's anger seemed to suddenly fade

away. He slumped down into a chair, carved from an old tree root, and looked defeated. He sighed heavily. "I suppose someone was going to find me sooner or later." His hands crackled with energy as he spoke.

"We were told in the village that you had been killed by the storm," said Zia. "Everyone thought that you had been hit by lightning and died on the mountain."

"I often think it would have been better if the lightning had killed me," said Neil Robertson. "Instead it turned me into this ... monster."

"What do you mean?" asked Max. He and Li had been standing at the entrance to the cave watching while Zia spoke to the man in black.

"I was working on the mountain when the storm hit. I used to be a park ranger, you know. I've always loved this mountain," he told them. "The storm got pretty bad. Lots of people were in trouble and I was doing my best to help them all. However, there was lightning striking everywhere and one fork hit me straight on. I suppose I should have been killed, but I didn't feel any different. I couldn't get over how lucky I was, until I started to notice the change." He stopped and took a deep breath. "I touched a tree to steady myself and the whole trunk went up in smoke. I jumped back, shocked, and my hand touched another tree that also burst into flames. It was me. I had all this energy inside me that I was transferring to the trees and destroying them. I quickly realised that if I did that to trees, what would I do if I came

into contact with a person? I'd fry them! I just couldn't do that. I couldn't return to the town. So instead I made my life on this mountain. I found this old cave and made it my home."

"And you've been here ever since?" asked Zia.

"Pretty much," Neil told her.

"But people have seen you in the town," Max

pointed out.

"That's the other part of my curse," Neil explained. "A little while later, I noticed that my energy was wearing off. I was thrilled and thought that maybe I was returning to normal and could

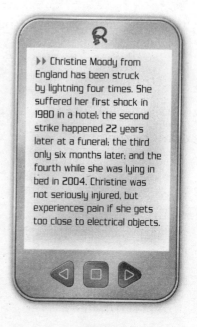

▶▶ Christine Moody from England has been struck by lightning four times. She suffered her first shock in 1980 in a hotel; the second strike happened 22 years later at a funeral; the third only six months later; and the fourth while she was lying in bed in 2004. Christine was not seriously injured, but experiences pain if she gets too close to electrical objects.

go back to my old life. But then I started to feel ill. It started to feel as if I was run down. I could understand that, my body had been through a big shock, but then it got worse. I could hardly walk or stand, it really was like I had a battery that was running out. I staggered out of my cave and found an old generator abandoned farther up the mountain. I don't know what I thought I was going to do, but it turned out I didn't need to think. All I had to do was touch it and somehow I absorbed all the power that was left in the generator. I sucked it right up. Of course, it meant that I was back to frying everything I touched, but I wasn't scared that I might die anymore."

"So it's you who has been stealing the power?" asked Li.

"I'm afraid so," said Neil with a sigh. "That draining effect kept coming back, and I've been scared of what will happen to me if I don't 'power up' each time. For a long time I was able to find energy sources outside of town that wouldn't affect anyone and get my power fix from those, but eventually they started running out. I had to start to look for new energy sources and, of course, there were a lot of them in the town. So I started to sneak in after dark, when no one would see me, and I would be less of a danger to the people living there, and find power sources to feed on. I always make sure I'm wearing my rubber suits that would limit any energy transfer in case I do bump into someone."

"I'm sure if you talked to people they would be able to help you," said Zia.

"It's too dangerous," Neil replied. "I don't want to risk hurting anyone. I don't know how I didn't electrocute you when you brushed into me earlier."

"Z's kind of ... special," said Max, smiling.

"That's why I was so angry," Neil explained. "I didn't want you near here in case you got hurt. I don't want anyone on this mountain in case I can't control my energy."

"So you've been causing all the tree bombs to scare people away?" asked Max, looking impressed.

Neil nodded.

"There must be something that can be done to help you live normally," said Zia.

"No, there's not," said Neil, sounding angry again.

"Why don't you come to the carnival with

▶▶ In 1998, during a soccer game in the Democratic Republic of Congo, all 11 players on one team were killed by lightning. None of the other team was struck.

▶▶ Ray Cauldwell, a baseball pitcher for the Cleveland Indians, was struck by lightning during a game. He was knocked unconscious but came to and carried on playing – and was on the winning side!

us tonight?" Zia continued. "We can re-introduce you to everyone and I'm sure you'll be surprised."

"No!" Neil barked. "I am not going to the carnival. I am not going anywhere. Now I want you all to leave and I don't want to be in your database."

"But—" Zia was determined to help Neil.

"Let's just go," said Max, pulling Zia away. "If he wants to be alone, let's leave him."

9

Runaway Roller Coaster

"I just don't understand why Neil won't let us help him," said Zia when they were back outside.

'I've got a plan,' said Max. "If we're out of ideas, I can think of only one person who might have some."

He pulled his R-phone out of his pocket and texted back to base. He explained what had happened, and how Neil thought that he was beyond help and there was no hope for him, but that they knew there must be something they could do.

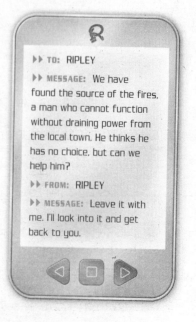

> ▶▶ TO: RIPLEY
>
> ▶▶ MESSAGE: We have found the source of the fires. a man who cannot function without draining power from the local town. He thinks he has no choice, but can we help him?
>
> ▶▶ FROM: RIPLEY
>
> ▶▶ MESSAGE: Leave it with me. I'll look into it and get back to you.

"Right, now can we go to the carnival?" he asked. "There's nothing more we can do until RIPLEY gets back to us!"

"I just don't feel right, having fun when Neil is cooped up in his cave," said Zia.

"RIPLEY will work something out," Max assured her.

The agents arrived at the carnival, which was already in full swing. Max pulled out his MFD glasses and put them on.

"Woah, the carnival lights look crazy through

these," he told them. "They look like you do Z, all swirling energy."

"The northern lights look pretty crazy without them," said Zia uneasily as she looked at the night sky and remembered what they had been told about the northern lights appearing 15 years ago, before the terrible storm.

"It'll be fine," said Max. "Now which ride should we go on first?"

"Hang on," said Li, suddenly. She pulled out the tin that she had put in her pocket in the cave. She had completely forgotten to put it back.

"What's that?" asked Zia.

"I don't know," Li told them. "It looked like a clue tin, just the wrong colours. I wanted to ask Neil about it, but I didn't get the chance."

"Open it," said Max excitedly.

Li gently eased the lid off the tin and a piece of rock fell out into her hand.

"Eugh," she said. "Dirt. Neil obviously keeps

his soil samples in here."

"No," said Zia. "That's volcanic rock. That rock is not found around here, someone has brought that rock from somewhere else. Hawaii perhaps? There are lots of volcanoes there."

"Maybe it's the first clue to Rip's next hidden artefact!" Max suggested excitedly. He took a photo of the clue tin and sent it back to the other agents at Ripley High. "Perhaps that's why the tin is a different colour? The red and yellow tins led us to Antarctica, I wonder where the blue and silver tins will take us? Now

▶▶ **TO:** Kobe, Alek, Kate, Jack

▶▶ **SUBJECT:**
Look what we found!

▶▶ **MESSAGE:** We think we may have found another of Rip's clue tins! Take a look at the picture, and the strange rock that was inside. The tin is a different colour, but do you think this is the start of another artefact hunt???

the guys back at base can have a head start working out where it has come from."

Max's excitement was soon dampened as rain suddenly began to fall heavily. A crack of lightning lit up the sky, brighter than the lights of the surrounding carnival. The storm Zia had been predicting had arrived. People began to run for shelter as the rain fell heavier and heavier and the sound of thunder grew louder in the sky. The thunder followed each flash of lightning almost instantly, which the agents knew meant that the storm was virtually overhead.

A bright flash lit up the night sky around them and then everything went dark, the flash had gone and all the carnival lights had died.

The RBI agents turned on their torches and examined the scene around them.

People were running around, scared by the sudden darkness, children were crying and most of the rides had stopped moving.

"What's that?" asked Li, listening to a whirring noise that was hard to hear over the noise of the crowd.

The others listened too.

"It's the roller coaster!" said Max shining his torch on the ride. The coaster was still moving. "The cars are still going around the tracks – they must be moving under their own momentum," he explained to the others. "Even though the electricity has stopped, the roller coaster has enough force to keep going by itself."

"Is that a good thing?" asked Li.

"No, it most definitely is not," said Max. "The cars are still moving, but with no electricity there is no way of controlling them and the brakes won't work without power. The cars will just keep getting faster and faster until," he paused, "they get up so much speed that they will fly off the tracks!"

"We have to do something!" said Zia.

Max ran over to the power unit that supplied the roller coaster.

"It looks like it was a direct lightning hit," he said. "I can repair it, but I don't know how long it will take." All three agents looked at the roller coaster, where the cars were speeding up around the tracks. People were screaming with excitement inside, not realising the danger they were in.

"See what you can do," said Zia, as she and Li stepped back to watch the coaster.

"Max, you need to hurry," said Li. "It's getting

pretty fast."

"I know," said Max. "But these circuits have been really badly damaged. I'm not sure even I am going to be able to save the power unit."

Li gulped and looked at the faces of the people on the coaster. Their smiles were now turning to fear as the roller coaster became dangerously fast.

"Look!" cried Zia, suddenly.

A bright light had appeared among the trees. It shone vividly in the darkness, and it seemed to be making its way towards the carnival.

"It's Neil," said Li.

"He's been hit by lightning again," said Zia, explaining the bright light that was surrounding their new friend. "He must have seen the lightning hit the carnival, and realised what might have happened. I bet he let himself get hit by lightning deliberately so that he could come to help the town!"

Neil arrived at the carnival. Terrified people

moved out of the way of the glowing man as he made his way through the crowd. He stood by the roller coaster, took a deep breath and then laid his hands on the track.

As the energy flowed out of him and into the ride the roller coaster lit up again, its lights working once more, and the runaway cars began to slow down until eventually they stopped and the people inside were safe.

"You're a hero!" Zia told Neil happily.

"I—" Neil started to say something but then couldn't. He dropped to the floor and collapsed, unconscious.

Regeneration

"What's going on?" asked Max, who was still working on one of the power units and had only partially seen what had happened.

"It's Neil," said Zia, "I think his power's run out. He used it all to stop the coaster."

"We have to do something," said Li, quickly. "Didn't Neil say that if he ran out of power he could die? We have to get him some energy – and fast!"

"I might be able to help with that," said Max. "I've got this generator back on line."

Zia and Li carried the unconscious Neil to where Max was standing, and placed him on the floor next to the generator that Max had mended.

Immediately Li heard the whining sound of

energy being transferred. Just being that close to the working generator meant that Neil's ability kicked in and the energy was able to flow from the generator back into him. Neil began to stir and then sat up, awake again.

There was a huge cheer from the crowd of onlookers who had witnessed the whole thing, and seen Neil save their carnival and many of their friends.

"I said you were a hero," Zia declared.

Two days later it was time for the agents to go back to BION Island.

"I think our work here is done," said Max with a grin as he watched Neil chatting to the town's people as they worked on his new house.

"I can't believe we didn't think of building a renewable energy house for Neil," said Zia.

"That's why we have RIPLEY," said Max.

"Now Neil can get all the power he needs without having to drain it from anyone else."

▶▶ A Montana couple have built an environmentally friendly house for less than $15,000. Their cosy home includes 13,000 empty soda and beer cans, and 250 used car tyres in the foundations. The savings don't stop there: by heating the house with a wood-burning stove and solar power, the couple's utility bills are only $20 per month.

He looked over at their friend who was smiling and looking so much happier than the man they had first met in the cave.

"Hey Neil," he called. "I've got a gift for you."

"Another one?" asked Neil. "You have all done so much for me already. If it wasn't for you I would still be a hermit living in the woods."

"No, I think you would have saved the carnival anyway," said Zia. "You're a good person and you would have come to the aid of people in need."

"Anyway," said Max, rolling his eye at Zia's emotional speech. "The renewable energy only helps part of your problem."

Neil nodded, he knew that he would still have to be careful about not over-charging himself and risking his energy affecting other people.

"But this is the solution," Max held out a watch.

"A wrist watch?" asked Neil.

"Sort of," Max explained. "It's something I created myself. My sister is diabetic and she has to constantly monitor her insulin levels. If they get too high or low she could be in danger – a bit like you with your power levels. I made her a watch like this that monitors her insulin levels all the time and beeps if they are not right. So a little bit of tweaking and, hey presto, this watch works the same way, and will monitor your energy." Neil took the watch, his eyes filled with tears.

"This is going to make everything so much easier," he told the agents. "Now I can live a normal life. I could even get my job back as a park ranger."

▸▸ Humans generate electricity. On walking across a carpet, our body can build up 10,000 volts, but because we can develop only a small electrical charge, the current released is not big enough to cause damage.

▸▸ Brenda Sheklian of California says that street lamps turn off when she passes and switch back on when she moves away. She also claims that her powers can turn off the TV and freeze her computer.

"Well, if you are going to be up and down that mountain, then you're going to need something to help you get around," said Li. She pointed to the electric buggy. "Why don't you take that? It'll save us having to take it back to BION Island."

"Really?" asked Neil.

The agents all nodded.

"There's just one thing," said Max. "I managed to repair all the damage to its internal circuits, but I had a real problem with the ignition. I just couldn't get it so that the key works properly. I'm sorry, we might be giving you a broken gift."

Neil looked at the electric car and the ignition

and smiled.

"I don't think that's going to be an issue," he said. He stepped into the car and put his finger over the ignition. At once the car started up and Neil drove away, back to the building work that was going on around his house, laughing and waving to the agents as he went.

"Do you think Dr Maxwell is going to mind that we gave away his golf buggy?" asked Li.

"Nah," said Max. He said he was working on a new one anyway. 'Faster than a race car', he said, don't you remember? That one was a bit slow anyway. Next time I'll just get him to lend me the new version!"

Zia smiled but wasn't sure that Dr Maxwell would be lending Max another of his cars anytime soon.

RIPLEY'S DATABASE ENTRY

RIPLEY FILE NUMBER : 56985

MISSION BRIEF : Believe it or not, power drains have been occurring in the Rocky Mountains along with unusual noises and fires. A strange man in black has been seen in the area. Investigate accuracy of these accounts for Ripley database.

CODE NAME : Electric Man

REAL NAME : Neil Robertson

LOCATION : Rocky Mts, Canada

AGE : 42

HEIGHT : 185 cm

WEIGHT : 80 kg

VIDEO CAPTURE

UNUSUAL CHARACTERISTICS :

Sparks fly from his fingertips, is able to start fires with a touch and can absorb huge amounts of energy. Tends to dress in black rubber clothes.

RBI DATABASE APPROVED!

INVESTIGATING AGENTS :

Max Johnson, Zia Mendoza, Li Yong

▶▶ YOUR NEXT ASSIGNMENT

JOIN THE RBI IN THEIR NEXT ADVENTURE!

The Lost Island

Prologue

The sun had not long been up and was gaining strength as it beamed down on a small village near the coast of Tanzania, in Africa. A young boy began his daily walk to the schoolhouse, as he did every day. He knew the way well and there was no reason for him to suspect that this morning's walk would be any different from the trip he took to school every morning. As he walked he listened to the sounds around him and noticed that something was different. The bird calls were not the same as every other day; something must have spooked them. The grass in the scrubland he walked through had been crushed, as if a herd of rhinos had run across it. Then, as he was studying the trampled ground, something caught his eye. He looked up in time to see a large shape rush out in front of him and stop for a moment before disappearing again behind a large bush. The boy dropped his school bag in shock, but then tried to calm himself. He rubbed his eyes, not quite believing what he had seen. At first glance it had appeared that the creature might have been an elephant; the boy quite often saw elephants not far from his village, so this would have been nothing unusual, but the creature seemed to have been covered in thick reddish-brown fur. He had never seen a fur-covered elephant before. He moved towards the bush where the creature had disappeared, hoping to get another look, when a horrendous noise tore through the strangely quiet air. He covered his ears, quickly. The sound was like nothing he had heard before, it sounded pained and menacing at the same time and he was not sure he wanted to know what could have possibly made it. The boy stood still for a second, filled with fear and unsure what to do, but then the terrible noise came again and the bushes rustled as if the creature responsible might appear and head towards him. In his mind something that made such a ferocious noise would surely eat people! As the sound filled the air for a third time, the boy could take no more. He willed his feet to move and ran as fast as he could back towards the village to tell everyone what he had seen and heard.

▶▶

ENTER THE STRANGE WORLD OF RIPLEY'S ...

>> Believe it or not, there is a lot of truth in this remarkable tale. The Ripley's team travels the globe to track down true stories that will amaze you. Read on to find out about real Ripley's case files and discover incredible facts about some of the extraordinary people and places in our world.

Ripley's
Believe It or Not!®

CASE FILE #001

▶▶ PETER TERREN

credit: www.tesladownunder.com

Dr Peter Terren from Western Australia enjoys playing with lightning in his backyard. He creates wild-looking light sculptures, that use up to 500,000 volts.

▶▶ He uses an electrical device called a Tesla coil, invented by Nikola Tesla in the 19th century. It is an electrical transformer that generates extremely high voltages.

▶▶ The Tesla coil discharges electrical energy into the air, creating arcs of sparks, or plasma, that resemble lightning.

▶▶ By standing in a metal cage, or sitting in a car, Dr Terren is protected from the potentially lethal electrical energy.

▶ ROCKY MOUNTAINS

credit: © David P. Lewis - istockphoto.com

▶▶ The Rocky Mountains run for almost 5,000 kilometres from Canada to New Mexico in the United States, that's farther than the distance between New York and Los Angeles.

▶▶ The tallest peak in the Canadian Rockies is Mount Robson, which rises to 3,954 metres. It is one of the 20 tallest mountains in Canada. Mount Robson is famously hard to climb and it takes at least a week to reach its peak. Only 10 per cent of attempts succeed.

▶▶ In 1980, two skiers tried to become the first people to ski down Mount Robson from its peak. They left a helicopter at the summit but were forced to abandon the attempt early on.

▶▶ The first European to discover the Rockies was Francisco Vásquez de Coronado from Spain who travelled to the area in 1540. The mountains were home to Native Americans for thousands of years before that.

▶▶ The Rockies get their name from Native American tribes who lived there. French explorers reported the name in the 18th century.

▶▶ ZHANG DEKE

Zhang Deke from China can use his power as a human conductor of electricity to light up six lightbulbs simply by placing them on his head and ears.

Credit: Zhang Xiuke/ChinaPhotoPress/Photocome/Press Association Images

▶▶ As the bulbs light up, he is even able to control their brightness. He has also cooked a fish in just two minutes by holding it in his hand as the current flowed through his body.

▶▶ Zhang Deke first discovered his ability when he was 47. While changing a lightbulb, he accidentally touched a live wire, but instead of receiving a shock or being electrocuted, he felt almost nothing.

▶▶ In 1994, he was examined at the Chinese Academy of Sciences, where experts said he has an unspecified physical dysfunction.

▶ LIGHTNING

▶▶ A single lightning strike in Utah, in 1918, killed 504 sheep in one blast.

▶▶ In Uruguay, in 2008, 52 cows died at the same time when lightning struck a fence they were grazing near.

▶▶ Nine years after being blinded in an accident, Edwin Robinson of Falmouth, Maine, recovered his sight after being struck by lightning on 4 June 1980.

▶▶ Being struck by a lightning bolt wasn't that bad at all, according to John Corson, even though the bolt went through his body and then tripped three circuit breakers in his garage. Since it happened, the 56-year-old says he has been feeling positively energised – he even goes so far as to say he feels ten years younger.

▶▶ There is no truth to the saying that lightning doesn't strike twice in the same place. There is no reason why it shouldn't.

▶▶ In June 1987, lightning triggered the launch mechanisms of three rockets at NASA's Wallops Island, Virginia, launch pad. Amazingly, the rockets were originally designed to help investigate lightning in the atmosphere.

▶▶ MISS ELECTRA

Danielle Stamp, otherwise known as Miss Electra, dazzles audiences nationwide with an electrifying show in which she subjects herself to potentially lethal high-voltage electricity.

▶▶ Miss Electra sits on a giant Tesla coil, and allows two millions volts to pass through her and out of her fingertips, feeling no pain.

▶▶ During her show, dazzling sparks can be seen flowing through the coil and shooting out of her hands.

▶▶ She can power neon lights with the energy coming out of her body.

▶▶ Miss Electra has performed at Ripley's Believe It or Not museums and on the Ripley's Believe It or Not television show.

►► RIPLEY

►► In his lifetime, Ripley travelled over 750,000 kilometres looking for oddities – the distance from Earth to the Moon and back again.

►► Ripley had a large collection of cars, but he couldn't drive. He also bought a Chinese sailing boat, called Mon Lei, but he couldn't swim.

►► Ripley was so popular that his weekly mailbag often exceeded 170,000 letters, all full of weird and wacky suggestions for his cartoon strip.

►► He kept a boa constrictor 6 metres long as a pet in his New York home.

►► Ripley's Believe It or Not! cartoon is the longest-running cartoon strip in the world, read in 42 countries and 17 languages every day.

In 1918, Robert Ripley became fascinated by strange facts while he was working as a cartoonist at the *New York Globe*. He was passionate about travel and, by 1940, had visited no fewer than 201 countries, gathering artefacts and searching for stories that would be right for his column, which he named Believe It or Not!

Ripley bought an island estate at Mamaroneck, New York, and filled the huge house there with unusual objects and odd creatures that he'd collected on his explorations.

RIPLEY'S RBI FACT OR FICTION? BUREAU of INVESTIGATION

PACKED WITH FUN & GAMES, THE **RBI** WEBSITE IS HERE! CHECK IT OUT

REVIEWS

DOWNLOADS

MAPS & DATA

FUN!

MORE TEAM TALK

THE NEXT FILES

Check out the amazing, action-packed adventure with the Ripley team in ...